MR. BENNETT AND

MRS. BROWN

VIRGINIA WOOLF

ISBN: 978-1-963956-17-7

MR. BENNETT AND MRS. BROWN[1]

It seems to me possible, perhaps desirable, that I may be the only person in this room who has committed the folly of writing, trying to write, or failing to write, a novel. And when I asked myself, as your invitation to speak to you about modern fiction made me ask myself, what demon whispered in my ear and urged me to my doom, a little figure rose before me—the figure of a man, or of a woman, who said, "My name is Brown. Catch me if you can."

Most novelists have the same experience. Some Brown, Smith, or Jones comes before them and says in the most seductive and charming way in the world, "Come and catch me if you can." And so, led on by this will-o'-the-wisp, they flounder through volume after volume, spending the best years of their lives in the pursuit, and receiving for the most part very little cash in exchange. Few catch the phantom; most have to be content with a scrap of her dress or a wisp of her hair.

My belief that men and women write novels because they are lured on to create some character which has thus imposed itself

1 A paper read to the Heretics, Cambridge, on May 18, 1924.

upon them has the sanction of Mr. Arnold Bennett. In an article from which I will quote he says: "The foundation of good fiction is character-creating and nothing else.... Style counts; plot counts; originality of outlook counts. But none of these counts anything like so much as the convincingness of the characters. If the characters are real the novel will have a chance; if they are not, oblivion will be its portion...." And he goes on to draw the conclusion that we have no young novelists of first-rate importance at the present moment, because they are unable to create characters that are real, true, and convincing.

These are the questions that I want with greater boldness than discretion to discuss to-night. I want to make out what we mean when we talk about "character" in fiction; to say something about the question of reality which Mr. Bennett raises; and to suggest some reasons why the younger novelists fail to create characters, if, as Mr. Bennett asserts, it is true that fail they do. This will lead me, I am well aware, to make some very sweeping and some very vague assertions. For the question is an extremely difficult one. Think how little we know about character—think how little we know about art. But, to make a clearance before I begin, I will suggest that we range Edwardians and Georgians into two camps; Mr. Wells, Mr. Bennett, and Mr. Galsworthy I will call the Edwardians; Mr. Forster, Mr. Lawrence, Mr. Strachey, Mr. Joyce, and Mr. Eliot I will call the Georgians. And if I speak in the first person, with intolerable egotism, I will ask you to excuse me. I do not want to attribute to the world at large the opinions of one solitary, ill-informed, and misguided individual.

My first assertion is one that I think you will grant—that every one in this room is a judge of character. Indeed it would be impossible to live for a year without disaster unless one practised character-reading and had some skill in the art. Our marriages, our friendships depend on it; our business largely depends on it; every day questions arise which can only be solved by its help. And now I will hazard a second assertion, which is more disputable perhaps, to the effect that on or about December 1910 human character changed.

I am not saying that one went out, as one might into a garden, and there saw that a rose had flowered, or that a hen had laid an egg. The change was not sudden and definite like that. But a change there was, nevertheless; and, since one must be arbitrary, let us date it about the year 1910. The first signs]of it are recorded in the books of Samuel Butler, in The Way of All Flesh in particular; the plays of Bernard Shaw continue to record it. In life one can see the change, if I may use a homely illustration, in the character of one's cook. The Victorian cook lived like a leviathan in the lower depths, formidable, silent, obscure, inscrutable; the Georgian cook is a creature of sunshine and fresh air; in and out of the drawing-room, now to borrow The Daily Herald, now to ask advice about a hat. Do you ask for more solemn instances of the power of the human race to change? Read the Agamemnon, and see whether, in process of time, your sympathies are not almost entirely with Clytemnestra. Or consider the married life of the Carlyles, and bewail the waste, the futility, for him and for her, of the horrible domestic tradition which made it seemly for a woman of genius to spend her time chasing beetles, scouring saucepans, instead of writing books. All human relations have shifted—those between masters and servants, husbands and wives, parents and children. And when human relations change there is at the same time a change in religion, conduct, politics, and literature. Let us agree to place one of these changes about the year 1910.

I have said that people have to acquire a

good deal of skill in character-reading if they are to live a single year of life without disaster. But it is the art of the young. In middle age and in old age the art is practised mostly for its uses, and friendships and other adventures and experiments in the art of reading character are seldom made. But novelists differ from the rest of the world because they do not cease to be interested in character when they have learnt enough about it for practical purposes. They go a step further; they feel that there is something permanently interesting in character in itself. When all the practical business of life has been discharged, there is something about people which continues to seem to them of overwhelming importance, in spite of the fact that it has no bearing whatever upon their happiness, comfort, or income. The study of character becomes to them an absorbing pursuit; to impart character an obsession. And this I find it very difficult to explain: what novelists mean when they talk about character, what the impulse is that urges them so powerfully every now and then to embody their view in writing.

So, if you will allow me, instead of analysing and abstracting, I will tell you a simple story which, however pointless, has the merit of being true, of a journey from Richmond to Waterloo, in the hope that I may show you what I mean by character in itself; that you may realise the different aspects it can wear; and the hideous perils that beset you directly you try to describe it in words.

One night some weeks ago, then, I was late for the train and jumped into the first carriage I came to. As I sat down I had the strange and uncomfortable feeling that I was interrupting a conversation between two people who were already sitting there. Not that they were young or happy. Far from it. They were both elderly, the woman over sixty, the man well over forty. They were sitting opposite each other, and the man, who had been leaning over and talking emphatically to judge by his attitude and the flush on his face, sat back and became silent. I had disturbed him, and he was annoyed. The elderly lady, however, whom I will call Mrs. Brown, seemed rather relieved. She was one of those clean, threadbare old ladies whose extreme tidiness—everything buttoned, fastened, tied together, mended and brushed up—suggests more extreme poverty than rags and dirt. There was something pinched about her—a look of suffering, of apprehension, and, in addition, she was extremely small. Her feet, in their clean little boots, scarcely touched the floor. I felt that she had nobody to support her; that she had to make up her mind for herself; that, having been deserted, or left a widow, years ago, she had led an anxious, harried life, bringing up an only son, perhaps, who, as likely as not, was by this time beginning to go to the bad. All this shot through my mind as I sat down, being uncomfortable, like most people, at travelling with fellow passengers unless I have somehow or other accounted for them. Then I looked at the man. He was no relation of Mrs. Brown's I felt sure; he was of a bigger, burlier, less refined type. He was a man of business I imagined, very likely a respectable corn-chandler from the North, dressed in good blue serge with a pocket-knife and a silk handkerchief, and a stout leather bag. Obviously, however, he had an unpleasant business to settle with Mrs. Brown; a secret, perhaps sinister business, which they did not intend to discuss in my presence.

"Yes, the Crofts have had very bad luck with their servants," Mr. Smith (as I will call him) said in a considering way, going back to some earlier topic, with a view to keeping up appearances.

"Ah, poor people," said Mrs. Brown, a trifle condescendingly. "My grandmother had a maid who came when she was fifteen and stayed till she was eighty" (this was said with a kind of hurt and aggressive pride to impress us both perhaps).

"One doesn't often come across that sort of thing nowadays," said Mr. Smith in conciliatory tones.

Then they were silent.

"It's odd they don't start a golf club there—I should have thought one of the young fellows would," said Mr. Smith, for the silence obviously made him uneasy.

Mrs. Brown hardly took the trouble to answer.

"What changes they're making in this part of the world," said Mr. Smith looking out of the window, and looking furtively at me as he did do.

It was plain, from Mrs. Brown's silence, from the uneasy affability with which Mr. Smith spoke, that he had some power over her which he was exerting disagreeably. It might have been her son's downfall, or some painful episode in her past life, or her daughter's. Perhaps she was going to London to sign some document to make over some property. Obviously against her will she was in Mr. Smith's hands. I was beginning to feel a great deal of pity for her, when she said, suddenly and inconsequently,

"Can you tell me if an oak-tree dies when the leaves have been eaten for two years in succession by caterpillars?"

She spoke quite brightly, and rather precisely, in a cultivated, inquisitive voice.

Mr. Smith was startled, but relieved to have a safe topic of conversation given him. He told her a great deal very quickly about plagues of insects. He told her that he had a brother who kept a fruit farm in Kent. He told her what fruit farmers do every year in Kent, and so on, and so on. While he talked a very odd thing happened. Mrs. Brown took out her little white handkerchief and began to dab her eyes. She was crying. But she went on listening quite composedly to what he was saying, and he went on talking, a little louder, a little angrily, as if he had seen her cry often before; as if it were a painful habit. At last it got on his nerves. He stopped abruptly, looked out of the window, then leant towards her as he had been doing when I got in, and said in a bullying, menacing way, as if he would not stand any more nonsense,

"So about that matter we were discussing. It'll be all right? George will be there on Tuesday?"

"We shan't be late," said Mrs. Brown, gathering herself together with superb dignity.

Mr. Smith said nothing. He got up, buttoned his coat, reached his bag down, and jumped out of the train before it had stopped at Clapham Junction. He had got what he wanted, but he was ashamed of himself; he was glad to get out of the old lady's sight.

Mrs. Brown and I were left alone together. She sat in her corner opposite, very clean, very small, rather queer, and suffering intensely. The impression she made was overwhelming. It came pouring out like a draught, like a smell of burning. What was it composed of—that overwhelming and peculiar impression? Myriads of irrelevant and incongruous ideas crowd into one's head on such occasions; one sees the person, one sees Mrs. Brown, in the centre of all sorts of different scenes. I thought of her in a seaside house, among queer ornaments: sea-urchins, models of ships in glass cases. Her husband's medals were on the mantelpiece. She popped in and out of the room, perching on the edges of chairs, picking meals out of saucers, indulging in long, silent stares. The caterpillars and the oak-trees seemed to imply all that. And then, into this fantastic and secluded life, in broke Mr. Smith. I saw him blowing in, so to speak, on a windy day. He banged, he slammed. His dripping umbrella made a pool in the hall. They sat closeted together.

And then Mrs. Brown faced the dreadful revelation. She took her heroic decision. Early, before dawn, she packed her bag and carried it herself to the station. She would not let Smith touch it. She was wounded in her pride, unmoored from her anchorage; she came of gentlefolks who kept servants—but details could wait. The important thing was to realise her character, to steep oneself in her atmosphere. I had no time to explain why I felt it somewhat tragic, heroic, yet with a dash of the flighty, and fantastic, before the train stopped, and I watched her disappear, carrying her bag, into the vast blazing station. She looked very small, very tenacious; at once very frail and very heroic. And I have never seen her again, and I shall never know what became of her.

The story ends without any point to it. But I have not told you this anecdote to illustrate either my own ingenuity or the pleasure of travelling from Richmond to Waterloo. What I want you to see in it is this. Here is a character imposing itself upon another person. Here is Mrs. Brown making someone begin almost automatically to write a novel about her. I believe that all novels begin with an old lady in the corner opposite. I believe that all novels, that is to say, deal with character, and that it is to express character—not to preach doctrines, sing songs, or celebrate the glories of the British Empire, that the form of the novel, so clumsy, verbose, and undramatic, so rich, elastic, and alive, has been evolved. To express character, I have said; but you will at once reflect that the very widest interpretation can be put upon those words. For example, old Mrs. Brown's character will strike you very differently according to the age and country in which you happen to be born. It would be easy enough to write three different versions of that incident in the train, an English, a French, and a Russian. The English writer would make the old lady into a 'character'; he would bring out her oddities and mannerisms; her buttons and wrinkles; her ribbons and warts. Her personality would dominate the book. A French writer would rub out all that; he would sacrifice the individual Mrs. Brown to give a more general view of human nature; to make a more abstract, proportioned, and harmonious whole. The Russian would pierce through the flesh; would reveal the soul—the soul alone, wandering out into the Waterloo Road, asking of life some tremendous question which would sound on and on in our ears after the book was finished. And then besides age and country there is the writer's temperament to be considered. You see one thing in character, and I another. You say it means this, and I that. And when it comes to writing each makes a further selection on principles of his own. Thus Mrs. Brown can be treated in an infinite variety of ways, according to the age, country, and temperament of the writer.

But now I must recall what Mr. Arnold Bennett says. He says that it is only if the characters are real that the novel has any chance of surviving. Otherwise, die it must. But, I ask myself, what is reality? And who are the judges of reality? A character may be real to Mr. Bennett and quite unreal to me. For instance, in this article he says that Dr. Watson in Sherlock Holmes is real to him: to me Dr. Watson is a sack stuffed with straw, a dummy, a figure of fun. And so it is with character after character—in book after book. There is nothing that people differ about more than the reality of characters, especially in contemporary books. But if you take a larger view I think that Mr. Bennett is perfectly right. If, that is, you think of the novels which seem to you great novels—War and Peace, Vanity Fair, Tristram Shandy, Madame Bovary, Pride and Prejudice, The Mayor of Casterbridge, Villette—if you think of these books, you do at once think of some character who has seemed to you so real (I do not by that mean so lifelike) that it has the power to make you think not merely of it itself, but of all sorts of things through its eyes—of religion, of love, of war, of peace, of family life, of balls in county towns, of sunsets, moonrises, the immortality of the soul. There is hardly any subject of human experience that is left out of War and Peace it seems to me. And in all these novels all these great novelists have brought us to see whatever they wish us to see through some character. Otherwise, they would not be novelists; but poets, historians, or pamphleteers.

But now let us examine what Mr. Bennett went on to say—he said that there was no great novelist among the Georgian writers because they cannot create characters who are real, true, and convincing. And there I cannot agree. There are reasons, excuses, possibilities which I think put a different colour upon the case. It seems so to me at least, but I am well aware that this is a matter about which I am likely to be prejudiced, sanguine, and near-sighted. I will put my view before you in the hope that you will make it impartial, judicial, and broad-minded. Why, then, is it so hard for novelists at present to create characters which seem real, not only to Mr. Bennett, but to the world at large? Why, when October comes round, do the publishers always fail to supply us with a masterpiece?

Surely one reason is that the men and women who began writing novels in 1910 or thereabouts had this great difficulty to face—that there was no English novelist living from whom they could learn their business. Mr. Conrad is a Pole; which sets him apart, and makes him, however admirable, not very helpful. Mr. Hardy has written no novel since 1895. The most prominent and successful novelists in the year 1910 were, I suppose, Mr. Wells, Mr. Bennett, and Mr. Galsworthy. Now it seems to me that to go to these men and ask them to teach you how to write a novel—how to create characters that are real—is precisely like going to a bootmaker and asking him to teach you how to make a watch. Do not let me give you the impression that I do not admire and enjoy their books. They seem to me of great value, and indeed of great necessity. There are seasons when it is more important to have boots than to have watches. To drop metaphor, I think that after the creative activity of the Victorian age it was quite necessary, not only for literature but for life, that someone should write the books that Mr. Wells, Mr. Bennett, and Mr. Galsworthy have written. Yet what odd books they are! Sometimes I wonder if we are right to call them books at all.

For they leave one with so strange a feeling of incompleteness and dissatisfaction. In order to complete them it seems necessary to do something—to join a society, or, more desperately, to write a cheque. That done, the restlessness is laid, the book finished; it can be put upon the shelf, and need never be read again. But with the work of other novelists it is different. Tristram Shandy or Pride and Prejudice is complete in itself; it is self-contained; it leaves one with no desire to do anything, except indeed to read the book again, and to understand it better. The difference perhaps is that both Sterne and Jane Austen were interested in things in themselves; in character in itself; in the book in itself. Therefore everything was inside the book, nothing outside. But the Edwardians were never interested in character in itself; or in the book in itself. They were interested in something outside. Their books, then, were incomplete as books, and required that the reader should finish them, actively and practically, for himself.

Perhaps we can make this clearer if we take the liberty of imagining a little party in the railway carriage—Mr. Wells, Mr. Galsworthy, Mr. Bennett are travelling to Waterloo with Mrs. Brown. Mrs. Brown, I have said, was poorly dressed and very small. She had an anxious, harassed look. I doubt whether she was what you call an educated woman. Seizing upon all these symptoms of the unsatisfactory condition of our primary schools with a rapidity to which I can do no justice, Mr. Wells would instantly project upon the window-pane a vision of a better, breezier, jollier, happier, more adventurous and gallant world, where these musty railway carriages and fusty old women do not exist; where miraculous barges bring tropical fruit to Camberwell by eight o'clock in the morning; where there are public nurseries, fountains, and libraries, dining-rooms, drawing-rooms, and marriages; where every citizen is generous and candid, manly and magnificent, and rather like Mr. Wells himself. But nobody is in the least like Mrs. Brown. There are no Mrs. Browns in Utopia. Indeed I do not think that Mr. Wells, in his passion to make her what she ought to be, would waste a thought upon her as she is. And what would Mr. Galsworthy see? Can we doubt that the walls of Doulton's factory would take his fancy? There are women in that factory who make twenty-five dozen earthenware pots every day. There are mothers in the Mile End Road who depend upon the farthings which those women earn. But there are employers in Surrey who are even now smoking rich cigars while the nightingale sings. Burning with indignation, stuffed with information, arraigning civilisation, Mr. Galsworthy would only see in Mrs. Brown a pot broken on the wheel and thrown into the corner.

Mr. Bennett, alone of the Edwardians, would keep his eyes in the carriage. He, indeed, would observe every detail with immense care. He would notice the advertisements; the pictures of Swanage and Portsmouth; the way in which the cushion bulged between the buttons; how Mrs. Brown wore a brooch which had cost three-and-ten-three at Whitworth's bazaar; and had mended both gloves—indeed the thumb of the left-hand glove had been replaced. And he would observe, at length, how this was the non-stop train from Windsor which calls at Richmond for the convenience of middle-class residents, who can afford to go to the theatre but have not reached the social rank which can afford motor-cars, though it is true, there are occasions (he would tell us what), when they hire them from a company (he would tell us which). And so he would gradually sidle sedately towards Mrs. Brown, and would remark how she had been left a little copyhold, not freehold, property at Datchet, which, however, was mortgaged to Mr. Bungay the solicitor—but why should I presume to invent Mr. Bennett? Does not Mr. Bennett write novels himself? I will open the first book that chance puts in my way—Hilda Lessways. Let us see how he makes us feel that Hilda is real, true, and convincing, as a novelist should. She shut the door in a soft, controlled way, which showed the constraint of her relations with her mother. She was fond of reading Maud; she was endowed with the power to feel intensely. So far, so good; in his leisurely, surefooted way Mr. Bennett is trying in these first pages, where every touch is important, to show us the kind of girl she was.

But then he begins to describe, not Hilda Lessways, but the view from her bedroom window, the excuse being that Mr. Skellorn, the man who collects rents, is coming along that way. Mr. Bennett proceeds:

"The bailiwick of Turnhill lay behind her;

and all the murky district of the Five Towns, of which Turnhill is the northern outpost, lay to the south. At the foot of Chatterley Wood the canal wound in large curves on its way towards the undefiled plains of Cheshire and the sea. On the canal-side, exactly opposite to Hilda's window, was a flour-mill, that sometimes made nearly as much smoke as the kilns and the chimneys closing the prospect on either hand. From the flour-mill a bricked path, which separated a considerable row of new cottages from their appurtenant gardens, led straight into Lessways Street, in front of Mrs. Lessways' house. By this path Mr. Skellorn should have arrived, for he inhabited the farthest of the cottages."

One line of insight would have done more than all those lines of description; but let them pass as the necessary drudgery of the novelist. And now—where is Hilda? Alas. Hilda is still looking out of the window. Passionate and dissatisfied as she was, she was a girl with an eye for houses. She often compared this old Mr. Skellorn with the villas she saw from her bedroom window. Therefore the villas must be described. Mr. Bennett proceeds:

"The row was called Freehold Villas: a consciously proud name in a district where much of the land was copyhold and could only change owners subject to the payment of 'fines,' and to the feudal consent of a 'court' presided over by the agent of a lord of the manor. Most of the dwellings were owned by their occupiers, who, each an absolute monarch of the soil, niggled in his sooty garden of an evening amid the flutter of drying shirts and towels. Freehold Villas symbolised the final triumph of Victorian economics, the apotheosis of the prudent and industrious artisan. It corresponded with a Building Society Secretary's dream of paradise. And indeed it was a very real achievement. Nevertheless, Hilda's irrational contempt would not admit this."

Heaven be praised, we cry! At last we are coming to Hilda herself. But not so fast. Hilda may have been this, that, and the other; but Hilda not only looked at houses, and thought of houses; Hilda lived in a house. And what sort of a house did Hilda live in? Mr. Bennett proceeds:

"It was one of the two middle houses of a detached terrace of four houses built by her grandfather Lessways, the teapot manufacturer; it was the chief of the four, obviously the habitation of the proprietor of the terrace. One of the corner houses comprised a grocer's shop, and this house had been robbed of its just proportion of garden so that the seigneurial garden-plot might be triflingly larger than the other. The terrace was not a terrace of cottages, but of houses rated at from twenty-six to thirty-six pounds a year; beyond the means of artisans and petty insurance agents and rent-collectors. And further, it was well built, generously built; and its architecture, though debased, showed some faint traces of Georgian amenity. It was admittedly the best row of houses in that newly settled quarter of the town. In coming to it out of Freehold Villas Mr. Skellorn obviously came to something superior, wider, more liberal. Suddenly Hilda heard her mother's voice...."

But we cannot hear her mother's voice, or Hilda's voice; we can only hear Mr. Bennett's voice telling us facts about rents and freeholds and copyholds and fines. What can Mr. Bennett be about? I have formed my own opinion of what Mr. Bennett is about—he is trying to make us imagine for him; he is trying to hypnotise us into the belief that, because he has made a house, there must be a person living there. With all his powers of observation, which are marvellous, with all his sympathy and humanity, which are great, Mr. Bennett has never once looked at Mrs.

Brown in her corner. There she sits in the corner of the carriage—that carriage which is travelling, not from Richmond to Waterloo, but from one age of English literature to the next, for Mrs. Brown is eternal, Mrs. Brown is human nature, Mrs. Brown changes only on the surface, it is the novelists who get in and out—there she sits and not one of the Edwardian writers has so much as looked at her. They have looked very powerfully, searchingly, and sympathetically out of the window; at factories, at Utopias, even at the decoration and upholstery of the carriage; but never at her, never at life, never at human nature. And so they have developed a technique of novel-writing which suits their purpose; they have made tools and established conventions which do their business. But those tools are not our tools, and that business is not our business. For us those conventions are ruin, those tools are death.

You may well complain of the vagueness of my language. What is a convention, a tool, you may ask, and what do you mean by saying that Mr. Bennett's and Mr. Wells's and Mr. Galsworthy's conventions are the wrong conventions for the Georgian's? The question is difficult: I will attempt a short cut. A convention in writing is not much different from a convention in manners. Both in life and in literature it is necessary to have some means of bridging the gulf between the hostess and her unknown guest on the one hand, the writer and his unknown reader on the other. The hostess bethinks her of the weather, for generations of hostesses have established the fact that this is a subject of universal interest in which we all believe.

She begins by saying that we are having a wretched May, and, having thus got into touch with her unknown guest, proceeds to matters of greater interest. So it is in literature. The writer must get into touch with his reader by putting before him something which he recognises, which therefore stimulates his imagination, and makes him willing to co-operate in the far more difficult business of intimacy. And it is of the highest importance that this common meeting-place should be reached easily, almost instinctively, in the dark, with one's eyes shut. Here is Mr. Bennett making use of this common ground in the passage which I have quoted. The problem before him was to make us believe in the reality of Hilda Lessways. So he began, being an Edwardian, by describing accurately and minutely the sort of house Hilda lived in, and the sort of house she saw from the window. House property was the common ground from which the Edwardians found it easy to proceed to intimacy. Indirect as it seems to us, the convention worked admirably, and thousands of Hilda Lessways were launched upon the world by this means. For that age and generation, the convention was a good one.

But now, if you will allow me to pull my own anecdote to pieces, you will see how keenly I felt the lack of a convention, and how serious a matter it is when the tools of one generation are useless for the next. The incident had made a great impression on me. But how was I to transmit it to you? All I could do was to report as accurately as I could what was said, to describe in detail what was worn, to say, despairingly, that all sorts of scenes rushed into my mind, to proceed to tumble them out pell-mell, and to describe this vivid, this overmastering impression by likening it to a draught or a smell of burning. To tell you the truth, I was also strongly tempted to manufacture a three-volume novel about the old lady's son, and his adventures crossing the Atlantic, and her daughter, and how she kept a milliner's shop in Westminster, the past life of Smith himself, and his house at Sheffield, though such stories seem to me the most dreary, irrelevant, and humbugging affairs in the world.

But if I had done that I should have escaped the appalling effort of saying what I meant. And to have got at what I meant I should have had to go back and back and back; to experiment with one thing and another; to try this sentence and that, referring each word to my vision, matching it as exactly as possible, and knowing that somehow I had to find a common ground between us, a convention which would not seem to you too odd, unreal, and far-fetched to believe in. I admit that I shirked that arduous undertaking. I let my Mrs. Brown slip through my fingers. I have told you nothing whatever about her. But that is partly the great Edwardians' fault. I asked them—they are my elders and betters—How shall I begin to describe this woman's character? And they said, "Begin by saying that her father kept a shop in Harrogate. Ascertain the rent. Ascertain the wages of shop assistants in the year 1878. Discover what her mother died of. Describe cancer. Describe calico. Describe——" But I cried, "Stop! Stop!" And I regret to say that I threw that ugly, that clumsy, that incongruous tool out of the window, for I knew that if I began describing the cancer and the calico, my Mrs. Brown, that vision to which I cling though I know no way of imparting it to you, would have been dulled and tarnished and vanished for ever.

That is what I mean by saying that the Edwardian tools are the wrong ones for us to use. They have laid an enormous stress upon the fabric of things. They have given us a house in the hope that we may be able to deduce the human beings who live there. To give them their due, they have made that house much better worth living in. But if you hold that novels are in the first place about people, and only in the second about the houses they live in, that is the wrong way to set about it. Therefore, you see, the Georgian writer had to begin by throwing away the method that was in use at the moment. He was left alone there facing Mrs. Brown without any method of conveying her to the reader. But that is inaccurate. A writer is never alone. There is always the public with him—if not on the same seat, at least in the compartment next door. Now the public is a strange travelling companion. In England it is a very suggestible and docile creature, which, once you get it to attend, will believe implicitly what it is told for a certain number of years. If you say to the public with sufficient conviction, "All women have tails, and all men humps," it will actually learn to see women with tails and men with humps, and will think it very revolutionary and probably improper if you say "Nonsense. Monkeys have tails and camels humps. But men and women have brains, and they have hearts; they think and they feel,"—that will seem to it a bad joke, and an improper one into the bargain.

But to return. Here is the British public sitting by the writer's side and saying in its vast and unanimous way, "Old women have houses. They have fathers. They have incomes. They have servants. They have hot water bottles. That is how we know that they are old women. Mr. Wells and Mr. Bennett and Mr. Galsworthy have always taught us that this is the way to recognise them. But now with your Mrs. Brown—how are we to believe in her? We do not even know whether her villa was called Albert or Balmoral; what she paid for her gloves; or whether her mother died of cancer or of consumption. How can she be alive? No; she is a mere figment of your imagination."

And old women of course ought to be made of freehold villas and copyhold estates, not of imagination.

The Georgian novelist, therefore, was in an awkward predicament. There was Mrs. Brown protesting that she was different, quite different, from what people made out, and luring the novelist to her rescue by the most fascinating if fleeting glimpse of her charms; there were the Edwardians handing out tools appropriate to house building and house breaking; and there was the British public asseverating that they must see the hot water bottle first. Meanwhile the train was rushing to that station where we must all get out.

Such, I think, was the predicament in which the young Georgians found themselves about the year 1910. Many of them—I am thinking of Mr. Forster and Mr. Lawrence in particular—spoilt their early work because, instead of throwing away those tools, they tried to use them. They tried to compromise. They tried to combine their own direct sense of the oddity and significance of some character with Mr. Galsworthy's knowledge of the Factory Acts, and Mr. Bennett's knowledge of the Five Towns. They tried it, but they had too keen, too overpowering a sense of Mrs. Brown and her peculiarities to go on trying it much longer. Something had to be done. At whatever cost of life, limb, and damage to valuable property Mrs. Brown must be rescued, expressed, and set in her high relations to the world before the train stopped and she disappeared for ever. And so the smashing and the crashing began. Thus it is that we hear all round us, in poems and novels and biographies, even in newspaper articles and essays, the sound of breaking and falling, crashing and destruction. It is the prevailing sound of the Georgian age—rather a melancholy one if you think what melodious days there have been in the past, if you think of Shakespeare and Milton and Keats or even of Jane Austen and Thackeray and Dickens; if you think of the language, and the heights to which it can soar when free, and see the same eagle captive, bald, and croaking.

In view of these facts—with these sounds in my ears and these fancies in my brain—I am not going to deny that Mr. Bennett has some reason when he complains that our Georgian writers are unable to make us believe that our characters are real. I am forced to agree that they do not pour out three immortal masterpieces with Victorian regularity every autumn. But instead of being gloomy, I am sanguine. For this state of things is, I think, inevitable whenever from hoar old age or callow youth the convention ceases to be a means of communication between writer and reader, and becomes instead an obstacle and an impediment. At the present moment we are suffering, not from decay, but from having no code of manners which writers and readers accept as a prelude to the more exciting intercourse of friendship.

The literary convention of the time is so artificial—you have to talk about the weather and nothing but the weather throughout the entire visit—that, naturally, the feeble are tempted to outrage, and the strong are led to destroy the very foundations and rules of literary society. Signs of this are everywhere apparent. Grammar is violated; syntax disintegrated; as a boy staying with an aunt for the weekend rolls in the geranium bed out of sheer desperation as the solemnities of the sabbath wear on. The more adult writers do not, of course, indulge in such wanton exhibitions of spleen. Their sincerity is desperate, and their courage tremendous; it is only that they do not know which to use, a fork or their fingers. Thus, if you read Mr. Joyce and Mr. Eliot you will be struck by the indecency of the one, and the obscurity of the other. Mr. Joyce's indecency in Ulysses seems to me the conscious and calculated indecency of a desperate man who feels that in order to breathe he must break the windows. At moments, when the window is broken, he is magnificent. But what a waste of energy! And, after all, how dull indecency is, when it is not the overflowing of a superabundant energy or savagery, but the determined and public-spirited act of a man who needs fresh air! Again, with the obscurity of Mr. Eliot. I think that Mr. Eliot has written some of the loveliest single lines in modern poetry. But how intolerant he is of the old usages and politenesses of society—respect for the weak, consideration for the dull! As I sun myself upon the intense and ravishing beauty of one of his lines, and reflect that I must make a dizzy and dangerous leap to the next, and so on from line to line, like an acrobat flying precariously from bar to bar, I cry out, I confess, for the old decorums, and envy the indolence of my ancestors who, instead of spinning madly through mid-air, dreamt quietly in the shade with a book. Again, in Mr. Strachey's books, "Eminent Victorians" and "Queen Victoria," the effort and strain of writing against the grain and current of the times is visible too.

It is much less visible, of course, for not only is he dealing with facts, which are stubborn things, but he has fabricated, chiefly from eighteenth-century material, a very discreet code of manners of his own, which allows him to sit at table with the highest in the land and to say a great many things under cover of that exquisite apparel which, had they gone naked, would have been chased by the men-servants from the room. Still, if you compare "Eminent Victorians" with some of Lord Macaulay's essays, though you will feel that Lord Macaulay is always wrong, and

Mr. Strachey always right, you will also feel a body, a sweep, a richness in Lord Macaulay's essays which show that his age was behind him; all his strength went straight into his work; none was used for purposes of concealment or of conversion. But Mr. Strachey has had to open our eyes before he made us see; he has had to search out and sew together a very artful manner of speech; and the effort, beautifully though it is concealed, has robbed his work of some of the force that should have gone into it, and limited his scope.

For these reasons, then, we must reconcile ourselves to a season of failures and fragments. We must reflect that where so much strength is spent on finding a way of telling the truth the truth itself is bound to reach us in rather an exhausted and chaotic condition. Ulysses, Queen Victoria, Mr. Prufrock—to give Mrs. Brown some of the names she has made famous lately—is a little pale and dishevelled by the time her rescuers reach her. And it is the sound of their axes that we hear—a vigorous and stimulating sound in my ears—unless of course you wish to sleep, when, in the bounty of his concern, Providence has provided a host of writers anxious and able to satisfy your needs.

Thus I have tried, at tedious length, I fear,

to answer some of the questions which I began by asking. I have given an account of some of the difficulties which in my view beset the Georgian writer in all his forms. I have sought to excuse him. May I end by venturing to remind you of the duties and responsibilities that are yours as partners in this business of writing books, as companions in the railway carriage, as fellow travellers with Mrs. Brown? For she is just as visible to you who remain silent as to us who tell stories about her. In the course of your daily life this past week you have had far stranger and more interesting experiences than the one I have tried to describe. You have overheard scraps of talk that filled you with amazement.

You have gone to bed at night bewildered by the complexity of your feelings. In one day thousands of ideas have coursed through your brains; thousands of emotions have met, collided, and disappeared in astonishing disorder. Nevertheless, you allow the writers to palm off upon you a version of all this, an image of Mrs. Brown, which has no likeness to that surprising apparition whatsoever. In your modesty you seem to consider that writers are of different blood and bone from yourselves; that they know more of Mrs. Brown than you do. Never was there a more fatal mistake. It is this division between reader and writer, this humility on your part, these professional airs and graces on ours, that corrupt and emasculate the books which should be the healthy offspring of a close and equal alliance between us. Hence spring those sleek, smooth novels, those portentous and ridiculous biographies, that milk and watery criticism, those poems melodiously celebrating the innocence of roses and sheep which pass so plausibly for literature at the present time.

Your part is to insist that writers shall come down off their plinths and pedestals, and describe beautifully if possible, truthfully at any rate, our Mrs. Brown. You should insist that she is an old lady of unlimited capacity and infinite variety; capable of appearing in any place; wearing any dress; saying anything and doing heaven knows what. But the things she says and the things she does and her eyes and her nose and her speech and her silence have an overwhelming fascination, for she is, of course, the spirit we live by, life itself.

But do not expect just at present a complete and satisfactory presentment of her. Tolerate the spasmodic, the obscure, the fragmentary, the failure. Your help is invoked in a good cause. For I will make one final and surpassingly rash prediction—we are trembling on the verge of one of the great ages of English literature. But it can only be reached if we are determined never, never to desert Mrs. Brown.